Let's Go Camping!

Heather Hammonds

Chapter 1

Outdoor Fun

Have you ever been camping? Camping is a fun way to enjoy the outdoors.

You can sleep outside in a tent. You can cook your food outside. You can play outside in the fresh air.

Many families go camping in summer. They like to go camping when the weather is warm.

It is fun to go camping with friends too.

Chapter 2

Places to Camp

People go camping in lots of different places. Some people like to camp in the **wilderness**. They enjoy the beautiful **scenery**. They listen to birds and see wild animals.

4

Some people like to camp at camping parks. They can use the bathrooms at camping parks.

Some camping parks have a shop and a playground too.

Camping Tip

You can find lots of places to camp on the Internet.

Chapter 3

Before You Go

It is important to make a list of things to take with you before you go camping.

Then you won't forget important things, such as your sleeping bag or torch.

Camping Checklist ✓

tent
sleeping bag
airbed and pump
torch
warm clothing
sunhat

cooking equipment
cups and plates
food and drinks
water bottle
bucket
sunscreen

Chapter 4

Setting up Camp

When you go camping, you need to find a good **campsite**.

Your Tent

Put your tent on some flat ground. Then the floor inside the tent will be flat.

Put your tent near some bushes. The bushes will shelter your tent if it is windy.

Don't put your tent underneath big trees. Branches might fall on it!

Don't put your tent too close to a river.
If it rains, it might get **flooded**.

This is how to put up a tent:

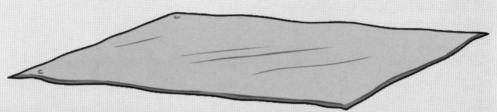

1 Put a **groundsheet** on the ground.

2 Lay the tent out on the groundsheet.

3 Hammer in the tent pegs.

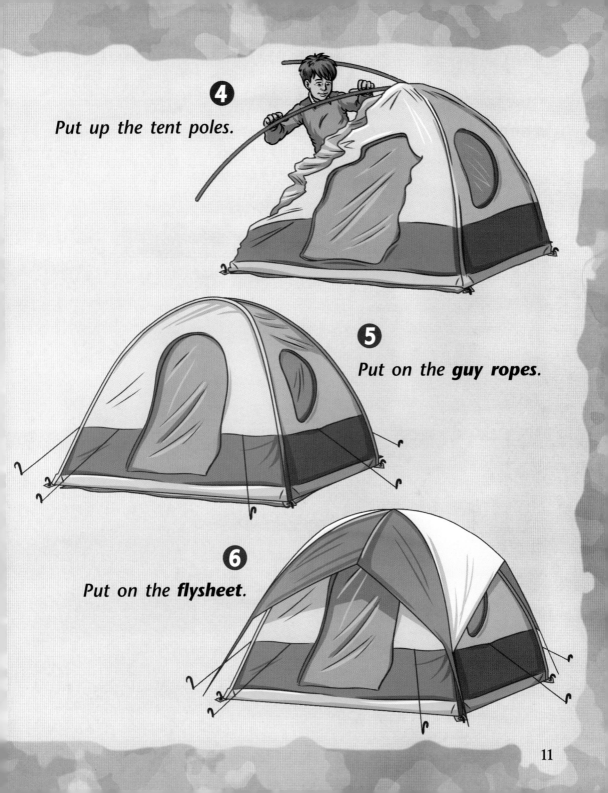

4 Put up the tent poles.

5 Put on the **guy ropes**.

6 Put on the **flysheet**.

11

A Place to Cook and Eat

When you go camping, you need a place for your camp stove, cooking equipment and food. Put them near your tent.

Safety and Rules

It is important to stay safe when you are camping.

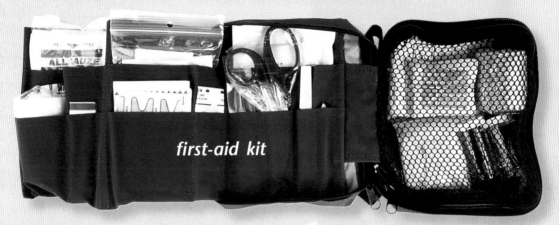

first-aid kit

Stay close to Mum or Dad when camping in the wilderness.

Keep Wildlife Wild

Always follow camping park rules.

Chapter 5

Camp Cooking

It is fun to cook outside when you are camping. You can help Mum or Dad cook on a camp stove.

You can cook lots of delicious food on a camp stove.

Camping Tip

Cooking on camp fires can be dangerous.

If a camp fire is not put out properly, it can start a bushfire.

It is safest to cook food on a camp stove.

Food

When you go camping, it is best to take food in tins or packets. Tins or packets are easy to carry with you.

Keep food such as bread and biscuits in containers, so animals and insects cannot get them.

Chapter 6

Camp Activities

After you have set up your camp, you can have some fun!

If you camp in the wilderness, you can go **hiking** with Mum or Dad. Hiking is a good way to see beautiful places.

If you camp at a camping park, you can play with the other children there. You can visit places near the camping park too.

Camping Tip

Take some indoor games with you when you go camping.

If it rains, you can play with them in your tent.

Chapter 7

When Night-time Comes ...

It is exciting to sleep in a tent at night. You can light up your tent with your torch.

You can snuggle into your warm sleeping bag.

Sometimes you can hear crickets in the grass outside your tent. You might hear a fox bark or an owl hoot too!

Camping Tip

Keep your torch beside your sleeping bag at night.

Then you will be able to find it quickly, if you need it.

Chapter 8

Going Home

At the end of a camping holiday, you must pack up your campsite.

You must take down your tent. You must pack away your cooking equipment, and your table and chairs.

It is very important to clean up your campsite before you go home.

Pick up all your rubbish.

Leave your campsite as you found it.

Camping Tip

Bring a big bag from home, so you will have somewhere to put your rubbish if there are no bins at your campsite.

Chapter 9

Camping in the Garden

You can have lots of fun camping at home.

Look for a good place to camp in your garden. Ask Mum or Dad to help you.

Then put up your tent, and your table and chairs.

Eat your dinner beside your tent. Play outdoor games.

Camping in your garden is good practice for when you go on a camping holiday.

Glossary

campsite	a place where you can camp
first-aid kit	a box containing things such as bandages and medicine
flooded	covered or filled with water
flysheet	a big sheet that goes over the top of a tent to help keep wind and rain out
groundsheet	a big sheet that goes underneath a tent to help stop the bottom of the tent from getting wet
guy ropes	special ropes that help keep a tent up
hiking	going on long walks, often in forests, mountains or other wild places
scenery	the view of the land around you
wilderness	wild places such as forests or mountains

Index